To my family
~N. G.

To Paul, with thanks
~M. T.

An Imprint of Sterling Publishing
387 Park Avenue South
New York, NY 10016

Text © 2004 by Nicola Grant
Illustrations © 2004 by Michael Terry

This 2012 custom edition is published exclusively
for Sandy Creek by Little Tiger Press.

ISBN 978-1-4351-0873-8

Manufactured in Heshan, China

Lot #:
4 6 8 10 9 7 5
10/12

Chameleon's Crazy Colors

By *Nicola Grant* and *Michael Terry*

Sandy Creek
NEW YORK

Deep in the rainforest all was not well. Chameleon was having trouble with his colors.

"Humph!" he said crossly. "I'm sitting on yellow flowers so I should be yellow. But look at me— I'm red!"

Chameleon hopped onto a stone,
and turned blue with pink spots.

Walking through the grass,
he went orange!
   It was all horribly wrong!

Monkey and Meercat strolled by. "You look a bit off-color today!" they said.

"I'm in a color muddle!" Chameleon cried. "I knew I shouldn't have eaten that funny-looking bug last night! What if Lion comes prowling? If I can't change color he'll see me and eat me up!"

"Easy!" said Monkey. "We'll help!"

"No problem!" said Meercat.

"Close your eyes and *think* yourself a color!" said Meercat.
"I am yellow, I am yellow," chanted Chameleon. He started pacing up and down. But . . .

"WHOOAAHH!"

Chameleon slipped on Monkey's old banana skin and skidded into a mango tree!

SPLAT! A big ripe mango fell on his head!

"Ouch! I *am* yellow now!" said Chameleon crossly.

"Well *that* didn't work! I need another plan."

"Easy!" said Monkey.

"No problem!" said Meercat.

Later, as Chameleon lay deep in thought on his favorite branch, two figures tiptoed up . . .

"Lion is coming!" they shouted. "It's LION!"

"Aaargh!" Chameleon tried to turn green—
but went purple!
     He leapt towards some purple flowers
to hide . . .

SPLASH!
Chameleon fell into the river!
Coughing and spluttering, he
scrambled aboard a floating log.
"Only joking!" shouted Monkey and
Meercat. "We thought if we gave you a
scare your colors would work properly."

That night Monkey and Meercat met in secret
to make more plans.

"What a great idea!" Monkey whispered.
"Let's do it!"

By dawn, the pair were ready for action.

"This disguise is *really* scary!" Meercat said. "The fright will definitely make Chameleon's wacky colors work!"

"Stand by!" hushed Monkey. "Chameleon's coming!"

"GRRRRR!"

With a great rumbling roar Monkey leapt out.

"Help, it's LION!" Chameleon gasped. He tried to turn green—but went red!

"Only me!" laughed Monkey. "Just trying to help again!"

"Great disguise," said Chameleon. "Shame it didn't work!"

But Monkey and Meercat wouldn't give up.

"LION!" they shouted as Chameleon munched his crunchy lunch.

Chameleon almost choked on his beetle. Instead of going brown, he went blue!

"LION!" screeched Meercat as Chameleon slurped a drink. Chameleon hid amongst some pink flowers. But everyone saw him—he was bright orange!

"It's hopeless!" Chameleon sighed.

"Hmm. Not so easy," said Monkey.

"It's a bit of a problem!" said Meercat.

Chameleon flopped into the shade,
feeling terribly worried. Nothing
worked! What would he do if Lion
really came?

Just then, Meercat and Monkey shot
past. They looked scared. Very scared.

"Lion!" they squeaked.

"Ha, ha! You don't fool me!"
Chameleon laughed. But just then
he heard a very loud GRRRRRR!

Chameleon froze. He looked up and gulped a big gulp. "GULP!"

Lion was towering over him!

"What are you?" said Lion, licking his lips.

"I-I-I'm a red spotted thingy," Chameleon stuttered. "No, I'm pink and purple. Erm, now I'm red and blue *and* purple!"

Lion looked puzzled. Suddenly Chameleon had a brainwave!

"I've got Funny-Coloritis!"
Chameleon told Lion.
"Swallow me and you'll
get an icky tummy!"
   "Funny-Coloritis?"
growled Lion, backing away
fast. "Are you sure?"
   "Oh, yes!" Chameleon said.
"Eat me and you'll end up
looking crazy colored like
me, too!"

"Yikes!" gasped Lion,
quaking with fear. "I'm off!"
   And he disappeared in a
cloud of dust.

"Three cheers for clever Chameleon!" laughed Monkey. "He's got rid of that Lion forever!"

"Hooray for Chameleon's funny colors!" Meercat cried.

And Chameleon was so happy he went pink with pleasure—with bright blue and orange spots, of course!